For those who persevere ...

So don't be discouraged if you don't smash the apple every time. Learn the fundamentals. Practice. You'll be amazed at what you can do.

—Jerry Kasoff, BASEBALL JUST FOR KIDS

D0101374

Loretta loved her son, Delmore. "A mere sprout. Well rooted. The apple of my eye" was how she described him. Loretta was a gardener.

Delmore returned her affection. "I love you more than my glove," he told Loretta more than once. He didn't mean a gardening glove though. He meant the stitched and sweaty-palmed kind that smelled like old leather. Delmore was a baseball fan.

Dog loved them both because that was his nature.

Golden Delicious

Transparent

Gala

Spartan

When Delmore was three, Loretta planted three apple trees. One for the past, one for the present, and one for the future, she laughed. Every winter Loretta clipped them and every spring she mulched them. In summer she soaked their roots and dreamed of apples. Loretta loved apples.

Pippin   Jonathan   Gravenstein   Russet

She loved apple shapes. She loved apple colors. She loved how some apples were tarter and crunchier than others.

But every fall Loretta filled her wicker basket with dead leaves, not apples from her little orchard. She became discouraged.

Things changed the year Delmore turned eight. He pulled his wrinkled ball shorts out of his drawer well ahead of baseball season. Loretta wheeled her barrow out from under the eaves long before growing season. Dog shed his fur because that was his nature.

The soil was warm. Loretta's trees were budding. Hope was in the air. Apples! She mixed compost and manure, wood ashes and bonemeal together in her wheelbarrow and shovelled the mixture onto the base of her trees. Her spade made a rhythm as she dug and flipped the mulch. One for the past, one for the present, and one for the future, Loretta sang.

Delmore practiced nearby with his ball and glove. He tossed a fly ball straight up and pounced to where it dropped, neatly into his mitt—such accuracy, such control. Throwing and catching were Delmore's thing. Batting was another matter.

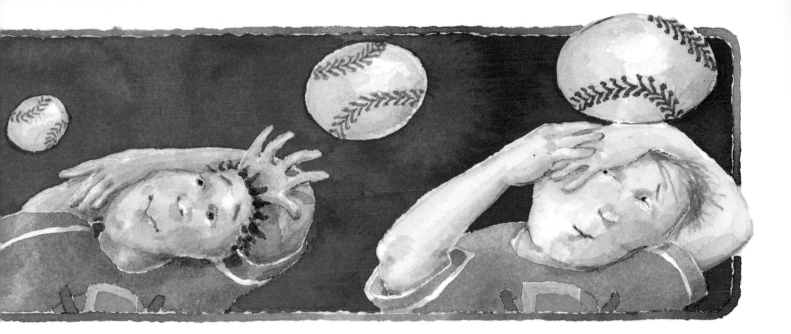

Batting was Delmore's stumbling block. Batting drove him batty. He felt himself useful with a glove and useless with a bat. His practice games with the Pee Wee Pitchforks were not going well. He couldn't whack the ball, hit a tater, smash the apple. When Delmore went up to bat it was a toss-up. Would the ball fly sideways? Upwards? Backwards? Would it knock the first base coach off his feet? No one knew for sure so everyone ducked just to be safe. Delmore had hit a lot of things but never a fair ball.

Loretta sympathized. She had grown a lot of things, but never an apple.

Dog sympathized too because that was his nature.

Spring arrived and nudged the budding trees into bloom. Each bud bore five scented blossoms that hummed with the activity of the bees. Loretta did a little last-minute pruning. One for the past, one for the present, and one for the future, snipped her shears.

apple blossom

honeybee

fruit spur bud

Loretta's focus

Delmore's focus

At the far corner of the yard Delmore pounded a plumbing pipe upright, waist height, into the earth. He propped his baseball on it. This would be his focus until he got it right. His bat would smack that ball until it dropped directly where he intended it to drop, even if it took months, years, his whole life.

Day after day Delmore and Loretta worked side by side.

Dog kept a watchful eye on them because that was his nature.

aphid

codling moth

tent caterpillar

Delmore swung at his plumbing pipe and Loretta checked her trees for pests. She pinched off any leaf that looked like it housed an insect. She painted the trunks with white lime to slow down the procession of ants and aphids.

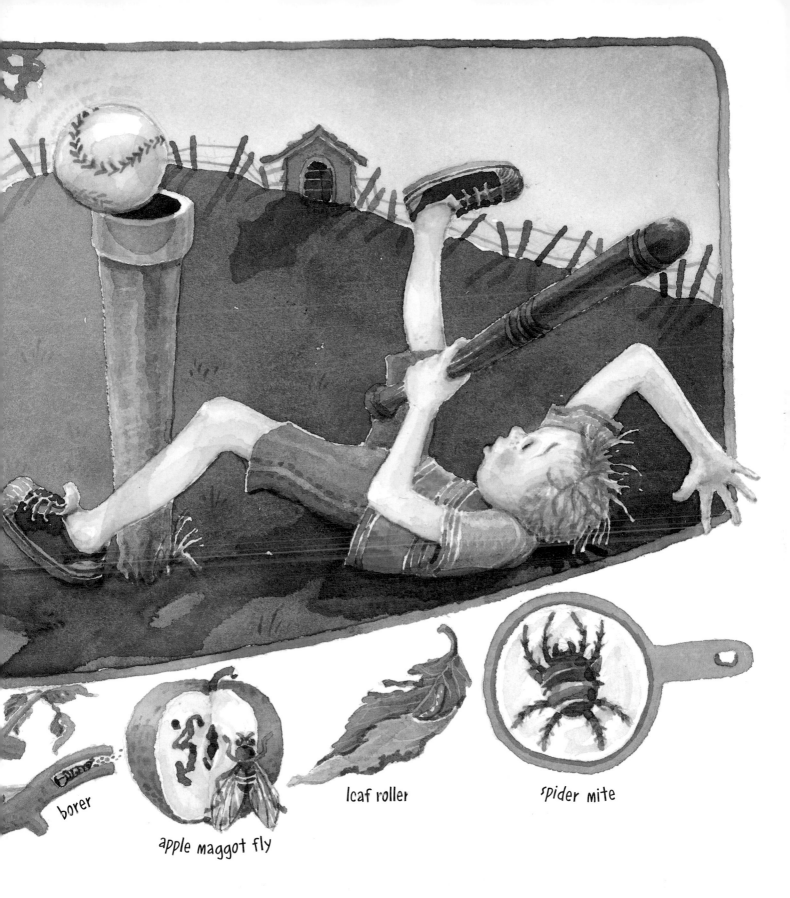

borer

apple maggot fly

leaf roller

spider mite

Delmore could see her in his outfield and imagined skipping a low ball past her, a well-aimed grounder. But instead he sliced air and twirled himself off his feet.

When Loretta found her first apple, she held her breath and touched it with her finger. It was a real apple. A baby apple! She ducked in and out of the branches of the three trees and counted five possible apples on the boughs. She was overjoyed.

Delmore was distracted for a bit by the sight of Loretta dancing in and out of her orchard.

Dog wagged his tail because that was his nature.

Then Delmore placed his baseball on his plumbing pipe and lunged toward it with his bat. He clipped the ball up past his own head, over his own shoulder into the brambles behind. He imagined his team members ducking on the sidelines. Oh, for a fair and forward ball!

The weather changed. It became as dark as Delmore's mood. His last game had left him frustrated. He had been up at bat with three teammates on base waiting for a good hit to bring them home. Instead he'd struck out. Again.

Only six weeks left in the season and Delmore still hadn't got a handle on his batting.

S T R I K E

It rained for a week. The water came straight down and leaked into Dog's house. It filled up Delmore's plumbing pipe. It knocked leaves off Loretta's fruit trees. When the sun pushed aside the clouds at last, Loretta went outside to see how her apples had fared.

There on the steaming grass beneath the trees were two little green apples. Now Loretta was left with three, dripping and clinging to their branches. Three stubborn apples, praised Loretta. One for the past, one for the present, and one for the future.

Delmore drained his plumbing pipe and set up his ball again. He stepped into his swing and let the bat follow through. The ball bounced past Dog's damp house. It's a breakthrough, thought Delmore—an almost straight-ahead kind of a hit. Dog was a witness.

Dog had faith because that was his nature.

One morning the wind took another of Loretta's apples. The past is over with anyway, said Loretta. I have two apples left. One for the present and one for the future.

Delmore's batting was improving. He held the bat firmly but not too tightly. His body and legs were alert but relaxed. His arms were out away from his body and his front elbow formed the letter "L" not "V."

Dog's approval was the silent kind because that was his nature.

But when Delmore mastered the straight-ahead fly ball, Dog woofed with pleasure and sprang into action. He played the outfield.

This was a mutually satisfying arrangement. Daring Delmore at the pipe clouted the balls closer and closer to Loretta's orchard, where they were hunted down tirelessly by Dog in the field.

Sadly, this activity led to the loss of one more apple. Delmore hit a line drive past Dog one afternoon. This ball, the fastest yet, ricocheted off the trunk of one of Loretta's apple trees and buried itself off to the side. Dog was confused and sniffed in circles beneath the tree. Finding no ball, he stood on his hind paws and delicately nipped a low-hanging sphere off the tree. This he returned to Delmore.

"If only dogs could see in color," sighed Loretta, rolling the rosy apple in the palm of her hand. "It is true though," she added, "that the present always gives way to the future. I do have one more apple left."

Polishing

Loretta gently
polished the last
apple. It was round
as a smile on the tree.

Delmore polished his
batting. A good swing was
no longer a pipe dream for him.
He was almost a slugger. With
just a bit more control, he would
bat with the best of them.

Dog lay low because that was his nature.

One late summer evening, just before the Pee Wee Pitchforks final game, Delmore stepped up to his pipe one last time. In the distance he could see Loretta's apple slightly swaying on its tree. It was a beauty, the size of a baseball now.

Delmore shifted his weight to his back leg and focused on the pale ball atop the pipe. In one fluid motion he swung his bat and sent his ball cleanly and swiftly in the direction of the last thing he'd looked at—Loretta's prized apple. He never expected them to meet.

Shortly after that Loretta's last apple said goodbye to its twig and went spinning over the garden gate.

Dog slunk under the porch because laying low wasn't good enough.

When Delmore showed
Loretta the bare spot on the
tree, he could tell she was
upset. For a few moments
she looked like she would cry.
Then to his amazement, she
started to chuckle.

"What accuracy, Delmore!" she laughed. "One apple for the future
and you hit it squarely and fairly off the tree!"

That night Loretta made apple crumble. Even Dog had a bite. It was so tasty that Delmore had three helpings—one for the past, one for the present, and one for the future, he told his mom.

His ball gear sat ready by the door.

The Pee Wee Pitchfork's final game was a good one. Delmore was quick in the field and Delmore showed fine form at the plate. He kept his eyes on the ball and held his bat sure and easy. Strike one—for the past! Strike two—for the present! But the third pitch was for the future and Delmore knew it. He met that ball just in front of home plate and sent it sailing over the outfield to the trees beyond.

The following fall Loretta harvested a dozen apples. One for each month of the year.

Up to Bat

Baseball Tips

- Face the plate.
- Place feet shoulder's width apart, with your weight on the balls of your feet.
- Turn face towards pitcher. Keep head upright, not tilted.
- Hold bat loosely with hands together on the handle.
- Raise back arm to shoulder level, parallel to ground, with elbow bent to form the letter L.
- As the pitcher winds up, keep weight slightly on back foot. As the ball comes towards you, take a short stride with front foot towards the pitcher.
- Pivot hips. Back toes should end up pointing at the pitcher. The pivot force from back foot, knee, and hips will carry arms out and around.
- Let the bat swing, but don't let go of it.
- Keep your eyes on the ball, stay loose, do your best, have fun, and don't quit!

In the Batter

Apple Crumble

1 lemon
³/₄ cup brown sugar
¹/₂ teaspoon cinnamon
¹/₄ cup water
¹/₃ cup butter

2 cups fresh bread crumbs (day-old bread cut into ¹/₂-inch cubes)
6 cups tart, firm apples (peeled and cut into ¹/₄-inch slices)

Preheat the oven to 350°F, and grease a round, two-quart casserole dish. Grate the rind of a lemon into a small bowl. Add brown sugar and cinnamon to the lemon rind; set aside. Squeeze juice from the lemon into a cup, add the water, and set aside. Melt butter and combine with bread crumbs. Layer the ingredients evenly in the casserole dish in the following order: one-third of the buttered crumbs, half of the sliced apples, half of the sugar mixture, the rest of the apples, the rest of the sugar mixture, and the rest of the crumbs. Pour the lemon juice and water mixture evenly over all. Bake for 40 minutes. Allow to cool before eating.